Yorkie Doodle Dandy

Yorkie Doodle Mystery 1

By Belinda White

Belinda White

Chapter 1

"I still can't believe you're taking Opie instead of me."

Amie gave an exaggerated sigh even as she folded another pair of slacks and put them into her suitcase. Things had changed between us since she fully came into her powers. She used to look up to me. I used to be the leading witch of our little twosome.

Not anymore. My magic couldn't hold a candle's flame to her raging inferno.

"I'm not taking him, Ruby. He's a presenter. You know that." She paused to turn toward me. "And I did try to get you a seat, you know. It isn't my fault they were sold out."

Yeah, who knew that a bounty hunter seminar would be so popular in the tri-state area?

"But I could really use it. Isn't there any way you can get me in? Maybe I could stay in the room with you guys and just listen in on the sessions from the hallway?"

Amie just gave me a look. Okay, that sounded wrong, even to me. But dang it, I wanted to know those new techniques in taking bond runners down too.

"Look, I've packed my voice recorder, and I'll record every session for you. That's really all I can do at this point."

Like recorded voices would show me the moves I needed to know. "Will you also promise to take notes and show me everything you learned when you get home?"

She grinned at me and crossed her heart with two fingers. "Promise. And if I miss something, Opie will be a good backup."

That didn't help matters, in my opinion, and I wasn't quite done yet. Mom wasn't the only one that could rack up the guilt level. "You do realize that you are leaving me here to prepare for the whole Fourth of July shindig on my own, too, right? That isn't really fair, either, just so you know."

That got me another of her looks. "You know as well as I do that our moms are handling most of that. We're just providing the space for it. Being the halfway point between them makes us the logical place. Not to mention all the outside space we have here to spread out."

She kind of had me there, but it brought up another good guilt-laden point. "All that means is that you are sticking me here to deal with not one Mom but two. That isn't fair."

Amie sat on the bed and patted the space beside her. I sat.

"I'm sorry you're not coming. When Boswell came up with this ticket and the offer for Opie to present at this thing, it was just too good to pass up. You know that, right? We're a team, and we need to keep up with things on the bounty hunting front. I'll share everything I learn as soon as I get back, and then you'll be all brought up to speed too. And now that we know these seminars are a thing, we'll watch for the next one so we can get plenty of tickets for all of us to go. Okay?"

I thought about it. Even if I protested more, it wasn't going to change anything. Sometimes life just wasn't fair. Take the whole awesome magical powers thing.

"Then I guess you'd better get downstairs. Opie should be getting home from work just about any time."

Amie threw her arm around my shoulders for a quick hug. "I'll bring you a souvenir if that will make you feel better."

Now there was a thought. Maybe I'd get something out of this after all. "I could use a new taser." Then I paused. "Or maybe another set of handcuffs?"

She laughed as she stood to finish packing. "I'll see what they have and surprise you."

I did like surprises. Maybe this wouldn't turn out so bad, after all.

A couple more items went into her bag, and then she took a last quick look around her bedroom. Everything that she'd laid out to pack was already in the bag. Amie shut it and then walked over to me, bag in hand.

There was another issue that I didn't bring up. I'd miss her. Yes, she'd only be gone a few days. But those days were in the middle of the week, and Arc had to work. I wasn't used to being on my own. I could probably count on my fingers the number of days that Amie and I had been away from each other. I know I could if I used my toes too. For an entire lifetime, that's saying something.

We both had our fellas now, and that was bound to change, eventually. That had been the main reason I'd been so gung-ho for all of us to buy this little estate. It was the perfect way to keep us all together, while still giving us the privacy we needed.

I was okay with her being in another house, although even that had taken some getting used to. But her being a whole state away was hard to swallow.

"You'll keep an eye on Destiny for me while we're gone, right?"

"Reowr."

And no, that last comment didn't come from me. It came from the little calico bundle of fur known as Destiny. I glanced over at the cat. "She probably thinks you should ask her to keep an eye on me." And truthfully, Amie had probably already done that, now that I thought about it. But I wasn't going to let that thought derail me. I had to establish some ground rules with the little Goddess-cat. "But perhaps she hasn't considered who would be responsible for dispensing food and water. Not to mention the whole litter control thing."

Destiny's eyes slowly turned to mine. There was a very calculating look in them.

Amie giggled. "Just try not to kill each other, okay? You know where her food is, and the litter too. I stocked up on both, so you should be all set until we get back."

I nodded, not trusting myself to speak at the moment. This shouldn't be this hard. It was only for three blooming days, right?

Belinda White

Chapter 2

Arc really came through for me that night. He must have known I was upset because he threw in an impromptu mid-week date night. We didn't have those very often.

Of course, it helped that I didn't have anything for dinner fixed when he came home from work, and that I hadn't really done any hardcore grocery shopping for a while. In other words, food was pretty scarce in the house at the moment. Something to add to my to-do list for the morning, but that didn't help us tonight.

But even so, I like to give credit where credit is due. See the best in people, and all that. So, in my mind, Arc totally took me out to eat to get my mind off Amie. It worked pretty well too. Food usually does with us Ravenswinds.

At least, it worked until he brought the sore subject back into the conversation.

"So, what are you going to do to fill your next three days?"

I took a deep breath. It was hard for me to

admit that I really relied on Amie as a guidepost for my daily duties. Whether I liked it or not, she was kind of the team leader right now.

"Well, I called Boswell and Vincent today, but neither of them has any open cases at the moment." Personally, I kind of thought that was odd. A part of me wondered if Amie hadn't told them not to give me anything until she got back. But that was just a gut feeling. No way to confirm it. But then, my gut is usually right. And it's just the kind of thing she'd do too.

Like I couldn't handle a case on my own or something. I so was up to that challenge. But if they wouldn't give me a case, I couldn't very well prove myself, now could I?

"You could go grocery shopping," he said, not meeting my eyes. "Maybe do a little baking?"

I laughed. Yeah, I wasn't a baker. "Don't worry, I'll go shopping in the morning. But don't think you will be coming home to all kinds of delicacies for the next few nights. You know my abilities in the kitchen are limited."

He grinned at me. "Yes, but it would be a prime opportunity to improve on that, wouldn't it? You could totally make up some cool snacks for the big party coming up. Show your mom what you're made of, and all that."

Arc had a point. It would be good to see Mom's face if I had a whole passel of delicious snacks already prepared when they got there. Still, it sounded like a whole lot of work too. And not pleasant work, either.

"We'll see. If I get totally bored, I might give it a shot." I hesitated. "Or, you could take the next couple of days off, and maybe we could go away too?"

He shook his head. "Nope. Not gonna happen. We're slammed at the firm right now. Dad and Uncle Merlin need me now more than ever."

I arched an eyebrow at him. "Anything I could help with?"

Arc swallowed and took a long sip of wine before answering. Like I didn't know that was a delaying tactic.

"I take it that's a no, huh?"

He sat the glass back on the table. "It isn't that I wouldn't want you to help me." Liar, liar, pants on fire. "But we're a legal firm. All of our records and files are highly confidential. We can't go showing them to anyone who doesn't work at the firm."

I opened my mouth, but he didn't give me a chance to get even a single word out. "And no, Dad wouldn't be willing to hire you on as a temporary. Besides, you've got enough on your plate with the whole bounty hunting thing. We still have to come up with that balloon payment for the estate at the end of the year, you know."

"But I've already said there aren't any cases

right now. What am I supposed to do with myself?"
Three days was starting to seem like an eternity.

"Maybe do some spring cleaning? Some yard work?" His face brightened. "Hey, that's it. You've been talking about putting in a flower garden. That would be perfect! Imagine how jealous Amie will be when she sees how pretty you've made the front of the barn."

The thought came racing into my brain like a runaway locomotive. "No. Not a flower garden. A witch's garden." I started bouncing in my chair. "Oh, that is perfect. And I know just the spot too. I'm sure Mom will let me get some plant samples from the farmhouse and the woods." I smiled over the table at him. "Thank you, Arc. You're just about the sweetest guy a gal could luck into."

He groaned. "You're going to want me to help, aren't you?"

What can I say? He knew me so well.

***

The next morning, I got up when Arc's alarm clock went off. That wasn't like me at all. But I knew how much work was in store for me in the next few days, and dang it all, I wanted that garden well started before Amie got back.

I wanted that garden to be a symbol of what I could do all on my own. Well, maybe with a little muscle from my man, Arc. But mostly, all me.

I'd made out my list the night before. I could pretty much get everything I needed from the farmhouse. And Mom would clue me in on where to get the rest. She knew things like that.

"Just don't forget to get groceries, okay? We need some food in the house. Today's a big court day, and I will be too tired to eat out tonight. Can you at least try to have dinner ready for me when I get home?"

With my plan in hand, I was feeling somewhat invincible. "Sure. I can do that."

"Good." He kissed me goodbye and left.

A glance at the clock let me know that I still had time to catch Mom at home. A short phone conversation later, and I had her full permission to gather what I needed from the farmhouse. She was giving me two of each plant and a small box of labeled seeds that she'd been saving for me.

I think I went up in her estimation a little with my request. And rightly so. I should have thought of this sooner. Every witch needs a garden. I knew I was starting the planting a little late in the season, but then my man was an Earth witch. I was pretty sure he could help things along a bit to make up for the late start.

If not, I knew that Amie could. But then that would defeat the whole purpose, so that most definitely wasn't part of my plan.

Dressed in cutoff jean shorts and a tank top, I poured a little kibble into Yorkie Doodle's bowl and topped off his water dish. Then I made my way to the farmhouse. Lucky for me, Aunt Sapphire and Uncle Archie had felt sorry for me being car-less and had gifted me Sapphire's old car when she bought a new one. According to them, they wouldn't have gotten much in trade-in value, anyway. They were probably right. My aunt was a lot of things, Goddess love her, but a good driver wasn't one of them.

The ten-year-old Ford Taurus didn't have a lot of miles on it and was in perfect running order. But you wouldn't know that to look at it. The poor car had definitely seen better days. Good thing I'm not too concerned with appearances, huh? At least not when it came to my mode of transportation.

Wheels were wheels.

I made quick work of digging up the live plants, and the seeds were right where Mom had said they'd be, waiting for me. It did me good to see the seed box with Amie's name on it still sitting there when I took mine. For once, I was ahead of her. I liked that feeling.

By eleven o'clock, I was pulling back into our driveway. Our resident ghost, Liz, was waiting for me as I got out of the car.

"Hey, Ruby."

"Hey, Liz. Everything okay with you and Patricia?" We didn't see as much of Liz now that her cousin, Patricia Bluespring, had moved her tiny home onto the back of the property. Liz spent most of her time there. Family is family, I guess. Even when you're dead.

She smiled at me. "Yup. We're good. I just wanted to let you know that there was a visitor while you were out. The lady from the library was here."

"Mabel Morgan was here? What did she want?" Even as Liz gave me a small smile, I thought of myself. "Sorry, I keep forgetting that you can't talk to regular folks."

"That's okay. I have all of you now. That's more than enough for me. But as for Mabel, I don't know what she wanted, but she seemed really upset when no one was here. She even went back to the barn looking for you all."

"I'll call her as soon as I get all this inside. Don't suppose there's any way you could help me carry them?" I knew the answer, but there was no harm in asking, anyway. Maybe things had changed since we last talked. Not that I thought that likely, but there were a lot of plants to carry in, so I still asked.

She grinned. "Not unless having a cheerleader would help you? Ruby, Ruby, she's our gal. If she don't do it, no one shall! GOOOO, Ruby!"

I was okay until she mimed the whole pompom thing. Then I lost it. When we were done giggling, she left me. Probably feeling guilty just standing around watching me work. I know I would if

I were her.

Once all the plants were on the barn's back patio, I brushed the dirt off my hands and went inside with my precious box of seeds. I didn't dare leave them outside until I was ready to plant them. Too many things could happen to the tiny little things.

When I reached my kitchen to wash up properly, I found an uninvited house guest waiting for me.

No, it wasn't a burglar or anything like that. Although when I got a look at Destiny's expression, I think I could have handled the burglar easier. Amie asked me to do one little thing for her, and I'd already screwed it up.

"I'm sorry, Destiny. I'm really, really sorry." I pulled out the small supply of cat food that I kept in my cupboard for her visits and poured her some in a saucer. Then I went to the fridge to get her some milk. That should make her happy. But there was no milk. Or anything else other than the pet food.

Once again, I'd forgotten about the shopping. Darn it. Now I would have to double back to town to get the groceries. And if I was going into town anyway, I might as well swing by the library and talk to Mabel in person. They closed from noon to one for lunch, and if I hurried, I might just catch her before she left.

Yorkie whined at my feet, then threw an anxious glance over his shoulder toward Destiny. I followed his glance to see Destiny munching on her food, her tail swishing wildly.

Yeah, that was not a happy cat.

Yorkie's eyes were pleading with me. I can't say that I blamed him. I wouldn't want to be cooped up with a ticked off Destiny, either.

"But I'm going to a restaurant for lunch. Restaurants don't allow dogs."

Another whine. And Destiny's tail kept slashing through the air. She would be done eating soon.

"Oh, all right. You can come." I'd work something out. We might have to sit out on the patio to eat, but we could make it work.

I hoped.

Belinda White

Chapter 3

I almost missed her entirely. She was just locking up when I pulled up to the curb in front of the library. Crazy Al was still preaching from his soapbox across the street. He'd toned it down a bit since all the trouble his sermons had caused last year, but not far enough down for me. The man needed to give it a rest.

Maybe even get off his soapbox and try to be a part of the solution. Not just yell at others to do the work needed to clean up the town.

Mabel started when she saw me getting out of the car. "Hey, Mabel, I heard you were looking for us."

She glanced around, then walked down the steps to my car. "How did you know that?"

Oh, yeah. Umm. "A little birdie told me?" Close, if not entirely accurate.

She just shook her head. "I'm sorry. Sometimes I forget that you all are witches. You'd have a way to know these things, wouldn't you?"

Her hands hadn't stopped moving since I'd arrived. She was definitely nervous about something. "You got plans for lunch? I thought maybe I'd treat you to some Carney's Pizza while we talked." I was hoping she'd agree because I knew for a fact that Carney's had outdoor seating. It was far too hot for Yorkie Doodle to stay in the car.

Mabel hesitated. "I don't know. Carney's is pretty busy." She bit her lip for a minute. "Maybe we could just grab fast food at a drive-thru and then eat here at the library?"

Something was telling me that it wasn't the time aspect of the crowds at Carney's, but the lack of privacy they would give for our talk. Something major was up.

"Sure, we could do that." I hesitated. "But I should tell you that Yorkie is with me."

Even her smile was nervous. "That's fine. It's the boss's day off. We can sneak him in with us to eat." Then she glanced in the car. "Amie isn't with you?"

I stood a little straighter. "No. Amie is out of town for a few days, but I'm here. We're all part of a team, you know. If you need help, I can help you."

It would have done my confidence a lot more good if she had looked a little surer about that. I really needed to work on my image a bit more. It wouldn't do to have the whole town thinking I couldn't stand on my own two feet.

I could. It was just more fun when I didn't have to.

It didn't take us long to get our hamburgers, fries, and drinks and make it back to the library. Mabel opened up one of the small conference rooms for us. You couldn't get more private than that. Especially with the library being closed and all.

By this time, I was fairly bursting at the seams to know what the bloody heck was going on. Did it have to do with her new beau, Tommy Hill? He'd been in trouble in the past. I was really hoping that the trouble hadn't resurfaced. If he'd started hacking again, it might have. The government was keeping a pretty tight rein on him.

I gave her the space to eat a couple of bites before I simply couldn't take it anymore. "So, what's going on, Mabel? Is it Tommy?"

She put her sandwich down and looked away, shaking her head. "No. I'm the one in trouble this time."

Mabel? The prim and proper librarian was in trouble? What did she do, jaywalk? It just couldn't be as bad as she thought it was.

I could have pushed her, but I'd already asked the question. The rest was up to her.

Finally, she reached down and pulled a packet out of her purse and laid it on the table between us. "Before you look at this, you should know that isn't me in the pictures. I'd swear that on my

Grandmother's grave. I don't know where they found someone that looked just like me, but they did."

My curiosity was definitely peaked. I opened the large brown envelope and pulled out two photos and a folded letter. The photos caught my eye first. They would catch anyone's eyes first. And I mean anyone.

The man in the pictures was out and out gorgeous. Strong, lean, muscles in all the right places. You could easily tell that because the man in question wasn't wearing a stitch of clothing. Neither was the woman.

And yes, the woman was Mabel. I swallowed, taking a closer look at the woman's face. She didn't just look like Mabel. I'd have sworn in a court of law that it was Mabel herself. Right down to the little beauty mark above and to the right of her left eyebrow. I glanced up at her face and then back down to the photo. Yup. Exactly the same.

Yorkie whined and then jumped on my lap. I thought for a minute that he was making a play for my food, having already snarfed down his own order. But he wasn't. His gaze was on the photos. Like me, he looked from the photos to Mabel and back. It was enough to make me wonder if maybe I hadn't been giving little Yorkie enough credit in the smarts department.

Finally, satisfied for the moment, he jumped back down.

"It looks bad, doesn't it? I mean, you think it's me, don't you? And you've known me all my life. If they can fool you, what chance do I have?"

Rather than answer her, or ask her one of the million questions that sprang to my mind, for once I did the smart thing. I unfolded the letter and read it. It didn't take long. It was short and to the point.

"Drop out of the running for County Commissioner, or I will post copies of these on every utility pole in town."

Huh. I hadn't even known she was running for office. Shows how much I follow local politics.

"Somehow I take it to mean that your campaign is doing well?"

She nodded. "It was until this. I'm up against Leroy Tanner. That man is despicable. His vote on town matters goes to the one willing to pay him the most. Period. I think the town of Wind's Crossing is ready for someone different in that seat."

I agreed. I might not keep up with local politics, but even I knew that Leroy was a no-good son of a buck. Having Mabel take his place in the circle of commissioners could only be a good thing.

"You think Leroy is behind these photos?"

Mabel hesitated but finally shook her head. "At first, yes. But then when I really thought about it, those could have come from any of the people paying him off too. A lot of things around here would change if I get elected. Some people wouldn't want that to happen."

She had a good point.

Okay, so what did we know? "Do you know the man in the pictures?"

"No. I've never seen him before in my life."

I looked from the photo to her and back again one more time. "I know you don't want to hear this, but I really think this is you in the photo."

She stood up. "Then I guess we're done here. I'll just have to wait for Amie. She'll believe me. Friends believe each other."

I gazed up at her and shook my head. "I believe you. I'm not saying that I think you really posed for this picture, or that you were even there at the time they took it."

Mabel slowly sat back down. "What?"

Taking a deep breath, I looked her in the eyes. "I've heard people can do wonders with photograph manipulation these days. I've seen where they have put people's faces into pictures that had nothing to do with them before. Usually, they make sure you know they've done it—it's a joke kind of thing. But someone who really knew what they were doing..."

She pulled the photos over to her and looked at them closely. "Photo manipulation. That would explain a lot."

"Yup. And I think Tommy would be a great one to help you out with this, truthfully. What with his computer background and all." I motioned to the pictures. "With his skills, he could probably do something like this in a heartbeat." I paused at her horrified expression. "I'm not saying it was Tommy! Nothing like that. I just think he'd be the one to ask for help, that's all."

Her horrified expression didn't ease off. "I can't show him these! What if..."

"He believed them? Come on, Mabel, Tommy is crazy about you. The two of you were meant for each other. And I really think he would be the one to go to."

"No. Absolutely not. I'll drop out of the race first." She stuffed the photos back in the envelope with the note. "I was miserable all my life until I got together with Tommy. I will not risk what I have. Not even the tiniest bit. If he saw these pictures, well, he could never unsee them, could he? Even if he believed me."

Ah. Okay, I guess I could see her point there. "All right. Then I'll check into it and see what I can come up with. But I'll need copies of those pictures. And the note."

"Do you promise not to do anything rash with them? I don't want anyone but you and Amie to see them. Can you promise me that?"

I thought about it. I didn't believe in making promises I couldn't keep. "I won't show the part with you in them to anyone without your express permission." I hesitated. "But I might have to show the man's picture around to find out who he is to get to the bottom of this."

Her eyes wouldn't meet mine. By the time they turned to me again, I'd already convinced myself I wasn't going to get the pictures. But she surprised me.

"All right. But I can only give you a few days on this. I can't risk them jumping the gun and posting these atrocities."

I looked at her. "A lot of people doctor pictures, you know. And a lot of people know you too. It might surprise you how many would stand behind you in this."

She gave me a sad smile. "You really don't understand politics at all, do you? Perception is everything." She paused before sliding the envelope back to me. "I wanted to be a part of the solution rather than the problem, but I'm not willing to risk Tommy or my new lease on life to do it. Selfish of me, but that's a fact all the same."

I took the envelope and put it in my bag before she changed her mind. Then I met her eyes one last time. "I'd like to ask a promise from you too. Please don't drop out of the race until you give me a chance to figure this out. I think we need you in that seat." I patted my bag, with the envelope just sticking out. "This only proves that."

Mabel thought about it and nodded. "I'll give you three days."

Chapter 4

My mind was racing all the way home. Part of me really wished that Amie was home to help with this. But part of me couldn't help but see this as the perfect opportunity to prove myself. To everyone. Even me.

Yeah, the last day or so had me doubting my abilities too. As I said, a lot has changed since Amie came into her powers. It would be nice to know that I wasn't so dependent on her after all.

I needed to do this. On my own too.

Yorkie started barking from the back seat as we left the town limits, but a glance out the window didn't show any animals or people in distress. More likely he just knew we were headed home and wanted a longer car ride.

Too bad, Yorkie Doodle. Momma has work to do.

When I made it to the back door and saw the

plants there waiting for me, my heart fell. Crapsnackles. I really wished I had waited before rushing into the whole witch's garden thing. But now that the plants had been dug up, it was kind of important to get them back into the ground as soon as possible.

They'd last the night, but tomorrow morning at the latest, I needed to replant them. The problem with that was that the ground had to be prepared for them first. That took work. A lot of work.

I put my bag on the kitchen counter and tried to get a handle on my priorities. Right now, I needed to come up with a plan of attack on how to handle Mabel's case. And technically, there was no reason why I couldn't come up with that plan while I measured off and tilled a little garden spot.

The little seed box still sat on the counter right where I'd left it. Seeds wouldn't be hurt if they didn't get planted in the next few days. I'd start with a tiny little spot for the plants and add to it next week. After all, establishing the garden was what really mattered at this point.

Luck was with me for once, and the small tiller in the garden shed was easy to get to, and there was even gas in the can to make it go. I really didn't want to make yet another run into town today.

I got the tiller ready to go, then carefully measured out and marked off the garden spot I had in mind with a ball of yarn and a few twigs. It was tiny.

In my calculations, I'd decided that a seven by five feet space would be more than sufficient to hold the living plants I currently had. I was glad I'd opted to start with one each rather than the two Mom had offered.

Still, that meant a dozen plants that would need room to grow. I'd worry about the space for the seeds once I got Mabel squared away.

My mind was working double time trying to figure things out as my body worked at making nice clean rows of tilled up dirt. By the time I had the little garden spot all tilled and ready, I even had the beginnings of a plan in mind.

I was feeling pretty darn proud of myself. Look at me. Getting started on a witch's garden, helping a friend, taking care of Destiny... there really wasn't anything I couldn't do if I put my mind to it.

Then the alarm on my wristwatch went off.

Amie and I had gotten into the habit of setting our watches to alert us a half-hour before our menfolk were due home. It had saved our bacon more than a few times. Hopefully, this would be one of them.

I stashed the tiller back in the shed and dashed over to Amie's house. There was no time for a run into town, and I'd promised Arc a home-cooked meal tonight. Things were not looking good.

Letting myself in her back door with the spare key, I immediately went to the fridge. Amie was a lot like me when it came to stocking up groceries. Which is to say, she didn't. Her fridge was just about as bare as mine was.

With little hope, I opened up the freezer door. Paydirt. A pack of hotdogs. Not exactly a three-course dinner, but I knew my cousin. If she had hotdogs, then somewhere around here, there would be coney sauce too.

I lucked out double and triple-time when I checked the pantry. Not only was there coney sauce, there was also a package of buns that didn't look to have any mold on them. Even if they were a tad bit on the stiff side. A few seconds in the microwave would have that stiffness out and they'd be good as new.

Then on my way out, I saw the finishing touch to my meal—a bag of potato chips. The Goddess must really be watching out for me.

Even with a simple meal like that, it was close. Too close for comfort, really. The hot dogs were barely in the water boiling when I heard Arc's car pull up out front.

Dinner would be ready within three minutes. You just couldn't time it closer than that. Feeling good about myself again, I met him at the front door with a big smile.

He did a double-take when he saw me. "What the... please don't tell me you need my help with a body."

I tilted my head at him in confusion. What the devil was he talking about? Then, out of the corner of my eye, I glimpsed myself in the entryway mirror.

Goddess, but I was a mess. My hair had bits of grass and dirt in it, as did... well, all of me. Crapsnackles. This wasn't the way I wanted my man to see me.

"I'm sorry," Arc said, leaning in to kiss my forehead. Quite possibly the one spot free of dirt showing right now. "I shouldn't have said that. It looks like you've had a full day. How's the garden coming?"

It was a nice effort, but once I'd seen how I looked, I just couldn't get past it. "Fine," I said shortly. Then I walked back into the kitchen and turned off the burner under the hot dogs. I pointed to the hot dogs, then took the small bowl of coney sauce out of the microwave. The buns and chips were on the table already. Kind of self-explanatory. "Help yourself. I'm going for a shower."

Arc looked at the meal and then at me. "Coney dogs and chips? That's your idea of a home-cooked meal?"

I'd had a rough day. There must have been a lot of emotion in the look I gave him because he backtracked. Big time.

"I meant to say, yum. Smells great. Can't wait to eat." He glanced at the food and then back to me. "Unless you want me to wait for you?"

I shook my head. "Nope. You eat. I'll be a while."

He didn't ask twice.

***

By the time I made it back downstairs, I wasn't feeling quite as emotional. And I looked a heck of a lot better too.

I found Arc in the living room, working on papers that he had spread out on the coffee table. "I hope you're not too upset, but I had to bring some work home tonight. We really are swamped." He motioned to the papers. "It was this or stay late at the office."

And he'd known I promised to cook. Even if that part was just left implied.

"Not a problem. I have some things to work on too, so it works out okay." I fixed myself a couple of dogs and ate them standing at the counter. When I was done, I noticed Yorkie at my feet, staring up at me.

When he saw he had my attention, he yipped, then walked to his food dish and yipped again. There was still kibble in it, but maybe he wanted fresh? I poured out a little more, but instead of eating, he yipped at me again.

"What?"

He started wagging his tail furiously. So hard his little hind end was moving. I still wasn't getting it. Sometimes I wished he and I had the same kind of communication that Amie shared with her familiar. It would be helpful in times like these. I mean, I could tell he was trying to tell me something. But for the life of me, I couldn't figure out what.

Arc came in to fill his glass with fresh water and glanced down at Yorkie, chuckling. "That reminds me of how Destiny reacts when she's ticked off. What did you do to him?"

Destiny! Crapsnackles! "He's fine," I told Arc. Then I picked up Yorkie and headed out the door. "We'll be right back."

Once we were out the door, I whispered into Yorkie's ear. "Thanks, little dude. I owe you one."

He chuffed in agreement. That, I got.

Belinda White

Chapter 5

The next morning, I got up with Arc's alarm again. He wasn't nearly as surprised as I was.

I'm not saying that I could get used to this early rising thing. It really wasn't my style at all. Hence the double-whammy surprise. But for the next couple of days, I saw it as a necessity. There was simply too much to do in a day if I didn't get an early start.

Being the nice girlfriend that I am, I let Arc take his shower first. Our barn only had the one full bathroom upstairs and a half bath downstairs. When he came back down fully dressed and ready to go, he found me at the kitchen counter making out a to-do list.

"A to-do list? Really?" He glanced over my shoulder at the list, but I flipped it over. I was kind of wanting to keep the whole case thing a secret until I had it cracked. "That isn't like you."

I looked at him. "And getting up at six is?"

"Point taken." He hesitated. "I kind of like the new you. Just asking, mind you, but is grocery shopping on that list of yours?"

I tilted my head at him. "Well, it needs to be done today, doesn't it?"

Arc grinned at me. "So, you'll add it to the list as soon as I'm gone, right?"

Dang, but the man knew me.

"Just make sure it gets added, please? We're pretty much bare bones in the kitchen, and a man has needs, you know."

Yeah, give a man a hot dog and next, he'll want a steak. Although, now that I thought about it, steak sounded pretty darn good. And they weren't all that hard to fix if I used the grill out back. Another item to add to the list.

He kissed the top of my head, looked in the fridge just in case some kind of breakfast food had magically appeared overnight, then left. Empty-handed. I think he did it just for show, but it worked all the same.

Grocery shopping didn't just make the list, it got the top billing.

Well, top billing on the list, but there was a timing thing involved. For instance, the local stores didn't open until nine through the week, and it would be another scorching hot day out today. Both of those combined meant that I needed to get those plants in the ground this morning.

Why shower before and after? I grabbed my gardening gloves and went to work.

Wouldn't my mom be proud of me?

***

The planting took a little longer than I had planned. It was ten before I was satisfied that I'd done all dozen plants justice and given them their best shot in their new home. The shower took a bit longer, and by then the day had already turned into a steam fest.

Shorts and a t-shirt it was. Not the most professional of attire, but it would have to do. A gal had needs too. Like not baking from the outside in.

The next thing to cross off my list still wasn't the store. I had to bypass that for the moment. A lot of things I wanted to buy would need refrigerated quickly in this heat, and I didn't know how long my visit with Tanner would take. Better to not take chances.

Because, yeah, I wanted to have a little chat with good old Leroy. Mabel might not be convinced he was the one behind the blackmail scheme, but I had my doubts as to his innocence. The man lived awfully well for someone on the county dole. Being a commissioner, from what I read in my research last night, really didn't pay all that much.

Certainly not enough to pay for the house in front of me. It rivaled Sapphire's new digs, and that was saying something. A mini-mansion rather than a simple home.

I walked slowly to the door, trying to think of a strategy. My mind still hadn't come up with anything by the time I pressed the doorbell. With as fancy as the house was, I kind of expected a maid or shoot, maybe even a butler to answer. But no, it was the prim and proper, not a hair out of place, Mrs. Tanner herself.

Her perfectly styled eyebrows raised as her eyes took me in slowly, from head to pink painted toenails. What can I say? It was sandal-wearing weather for sure. Toes had to breathe too. Well, sort of.

I should have womaned up and worn my leather bounty hunting get up. People respected me when I was in my leather. Oh, sure, sometimes there was laughter at first. But that generally faded out fast when they caught a glimpse of my taser and handcuffs.

"Can I help you?"

"I hope so. I'm here to see Mr. Tanner about a matter of some urgency."

Only half of her lips went into a smile formation. The result was a little condescending. Okay, a lot condescending.

"I see. Well, I'm afraid Leroy is out at the moment, but I handle a lot of his business. You can talk with me." Her eyes took a closer look at my shoes, probably looking for dirt or something.

She wouldn't find any. These weren't work shoes. They were for show shoes.

"Won't you come in?"

That was a wrinkle in my plan. I really wanted to talk to Leroy, not Mrs. Tanner. How could I get a feel for him if I didn't see him face to face? Still, at least I got in the front door. That was something.

"When will Mr. Tanner be back?"

She waved her hand. "Oh, it will be hours. He's playing in a golf tournament today. Tomorrow too, most likely. I'm afraid you're stuck with me. But I can assure you that I'm definitely the woman behind the man if you get my drift."

I took a closer look at her, then thought back to the last time I'd seen Leroy Tanner. There might be more than an ounce of truth in what she was implying. She looked all business. Leroy was more the playboy type.

As I still hadn't come up with a definite plan, I took a moment to look around as she led me to a sitting room. The room must have been where she did a lot of her business because it was decorated to impress. Did a pretty bang-up job of succeeding too.

The furniture was all black leather, and in the corner was an antique desk. The kind that probably had secret compartments to hold the papers Tanner didn't want to risk sharing with the world. Or, more to the point, the police in the event of a warrant. But what drew my eyes, as I'm sure they were meant too, were the pictures.

Pictures on the wall, on the tables, and even on the broad limestone mantel over the fireplace. And every single one of them showing Leroy Tanner in a prominent position with a celebrity or person of power.

Past presidents, television stars, you name it; they were represented well. Leroy Tanner got around.

I still didn't have a plan, and I was running out of time.

"So, tell me. What do you need from Leroy?"

All I could do was stall. After all, the only thing I needed from Leroy was a confession to trying to blackmail Mabel, and I was pretty sure she wouldn't be willing to help me with that.

"What do you think I want?"

She smiled at me again, her whole lips getting into the act this time. You'd think that would make the smile more genuine. You'd think that. But you'd be wrong. "I'm sure I don't know. But perhaps you wanted to put your bid in for one of the contracts that are coming open? The custodian contract for the courthouse, perhaps?"

Part of me was offended. She thought I wanted to be a janitor? So much that I was willing to grease the wheels to get the job? But it was as good an excuse for being there as any. So I played along, even if it did try my acting abilities.

"You're great at reading people," I said trying out a smile of my own.

She shrugged. "You get that way after dealing with the public on a daily basis." Then her eyes narrowed as she looked me in the eye. "That particular contract is quite popular, you know." A slight pause to let that sink in. "What do you think you could bring to the table to make my husband put his vote toward you?"

Talk about putting things right on the line. Mrs. Tanner was most definitely the woman behind the man.

As for me? I decided to play dumb. "Well, I'm a hard worker, and I cleaned my mom's thrift store for years. I know my way around keeping things neat and tidy. I really think I could make that courthouse shine."

Her smile was fading fast. "I see." The struggle was real, and it showed right there on her face.

Yeah, how could she be sure I wasn't some kind of sting operation to take down her husband's nice little enterprise?

Finally, greed won out. "Well, I'll have you know that my husband is as honest as the day is long." I had to bite my tongue to keep from laughing on that one. "But he does sometimes take my feelings and research into consideration when he votes to award contracts." She hesitated again. "I'd offer you something to drink, my dear, but I'm afraid my old refrigerator just isn't keeping things as cold as it should. I've had my eye on one of those nice side by side models with the metallic finish to match my stove. But on a Commissioner's salary? Well, it's quite out of my price range, I'm afraid."

We'd just bought one of those very models when we moved into the barn. They weren't cheap. Mrs. Tanner didn't believe in playing around. But the message was fairly clear. If she got her refrigerator, I'd get the contract.

Too bad for her I didn't really want it.

Chapter 6

So that was kind of a dead end, other than the fact that now I was pretty dadgum sure that the Tanners were behind the doctored photographs. They just had too much to lose not to try something.

And yes, my mind kept going back to all those framed shots of Leroy and the power people. Some of them just seemed a little too unlikely to be real. The only question was, did they do the manipulation themselves? Or was there some kind of dealer involved?

How good did one have to be to make a picture look believable? Was it something I could do?

Once again, my mind went to Tommy Hill. Mabel would have a cow if I brought him into this, but what choice did I have? I was okay with computers, but only for the simple things. Mostly email and web surfing. I was awesome at online shopping. But using special software to mingle pictures? Not so much.

If I got really lucky, maybe he could show me the ropes on how to use the software. Because right now, I wasn't seeing a way to take the Tanner's operation down that didn't involve getting Mabel elected. And she'd only given me three days to come up with a solution.

I would have to get creative. And I was nothing if not creative.

I changed direction and headed to Mabel's house. She should be safely out of the way at the library right now, and I really needed to catch Tommy alone for this one. I sat out in front of their house for a few minutes trying to figure out what to do. Finally, as much as I hated doing it, I tore the part of the picture with Mabel's face off.

Then I knocked on the door.

Tommy was a little surprised when he opened it to find me standing there. We were old friends from high school, sure, but after all these years, we really didn't spend much time together anymore. In fact, it was still a little surprise to me every time I did see him. Tommy Hill had been known as the fat geek back in the day.

Fat no longer applied to him, although he still earned the geek part. But now, he was totally the hot geek. Mabel was one lucky woman to have captured him.

But then, in my opinion, that luck ran both ways. Mabel was a fine catch herself.

"Hey, Tommy. Did I catch you at a bad time?" I had to ask because it was now going on noon, and the man was still just in his pajama bottoms. His short pajama bottoms, I might add. And can I just say again that yes, Mabel was a very lucky gal indeed.

"Hey yourself, Ruby." He glanced behind me. "No Amie?"

Why was it everyone assumed Amie would be with me? This whole being on my own experience was rather eye opening, to say the least. High time to work on my own independence.

"No Amie, just me. I've got something I'm hoping you can help me with."

He swallowed, and color came to his cheeks. "I'm really hoping that help doesn't require me to hack into anything. I don't do that anymore, you know."

I nodded. "I know. Government still keeping tabs on you?"

"You have no idea. I don't think I can go to the bathroom without them knowing. So whatever you need, it has to be totally on the up and up."

What could I say to that? My plan wasn't entirely on the up and up, but then did he really have to know that? I mean, I wasn't going to ask him for help with that. He would just be my tutor. And it wasn't against the law to manipulate images. If it was, the software wouldn't be so readily available.

"Can I come in?"

He glanced behind him, then stepped aside to let me pass. I'd been to Mabel's before. Not much had changed. Other than the hot new roommate, that is.

He led us over to the couch. "Can I get you a pop or something?"

I hated to drink their pop, but at the same time, I'd worked up a bit of a sweat on the ride over. The car's air conditioning worked just fine, but not on two-minute rides. No time to cool off the vehicle in that time. Not with the sun blazing through the windshield.

A minute later, we were sitting side by side on the sofa, sipping soda. Say that three times fast.

"So, about that help?" Tommy asked.

"Yeah, it's a bit of an awkward situation." I hesitated. Next came the tricky part. If Mabel found out that I'd come to Tommy, even without mentioning her, she would not be pleased. I didn't want to tick off my very first client. Even if I wasn't exactly getting paid for this.

Finally, I pulled out the biggest of the two photos, minus the incriminating female face. But before I passed it on to him, I looked him dead in the eyes. "You have to swear to me that you won't tell a single soul about this visit. Not even Mabel." Shoot, especially Mabel, but I couldn't really say that.

He fidgeted. "I don't have a problem with the secret part, though I'll admit I don't like keeping things from Mabel. But this is starting to sound like one of those can't do it jobs I was talking about earlier."

"It's not. Really." I started to flip the picture over, then carefully thought about his words. Saying he didn't have a problem with something wasn't the same as giving me the swear I'd asked for. "So, do you swear to keep this just between me and you?"

There was a second's hesitation, but he nodded. It was enough to make me glad I'd taken that safety second step.

I flipped the photo over. "I tore off the female's face. You don't need to see that, as it wasn't real, anyway."

He glanced at the picture in front of him, and his eyebrows rose. "I don't know, the rest of her looks pretty real to me. Pretty sure that body would come with a face attached to it."

"I'm sure it did. But trust me when I say it didn't come with the face shown in the picture."

His eyes went from the photo to me. "Someone pasted your face into this?"

Here's the thing. I don't like lying to my friends. So I shook my head. "No. Not me. But someone close to me."

"Amie?"

I shook my head but didn't say no. Amie would probably shoot me later, but I never once said it was her. I just didn't exactly say it wasn't. Tommy and I were friends. Good friends. But Tommy and

Amie? They'd almost been a couple at one time. And I knew within reason that there wasn't a whole lot Tommy wouldn't do if he thought Amie needed help. Government or no.

"I don't want to say who. The point of the matter is that whoever did this is trying to blackmail... my friend."

His face hardened right before my eyes. "That's not good. I'm not a fan of blackmail. At all."

"Me either. So, can you help me?"

He thought for a minute, then nodded. "The people monitoring my computer might think I've suddenly taken an interest in porn, but I'm willing to risk that."

The photo went into a scanner, and he popped open his laptop. It was already booted up and ready. I really don't think that laptop got much downtime. It's how he made his living, after all. Even if none of us was quite sure what the government had him doing. At least they agreed to pay him for it.

"This would be easier if I had the digital version of this photo, but we'll see what we can do." He starting pushing keys, and I watched over his shoulder.

"What are you doing?"

"A lot of the master photo manipulators out there are very proud of their work. They consider it almost an art form of its own. And sometimes it is. But anyway, as such, a lot of them sign their work.

I'm going to blow up the image and see if I can find it."

That sounded promising. A minute later, Tommy was pointing at the screen. "There. See it?"

I did. "Is that a unicorn?"

He nodded. "Yup. I've seen that signature before. I know who this is."

"Who?"

Tommy looked at me. Then he stammered. "Well, when I say I know who it is, I mean I know their work. They're proud of it. But I can't actually put a name to them."

I frowned at him. "Then how does this help us?"

He shrugged. "Well, now that you put it that way, I guess it doesn't." He chewed on his lip. "Back in the day I could trace them down, but now..."

"No. Absolutely not, Tommy Hill. I will not have you getting yourself into more trouble over this. We'll find another way to deal with it." I took a deep breath. "Actually, I kind of have a plan. But I need to know how to do what they did. Put faces where they don't belong. Is that something you could teach me to do?"

He took a deep breath. And then another before answering. "I can give you the basics, but this kind of thing can take a while to get really good at." One last deep breath. "It would be a lot faster if I just did it, but that would probably cross that very thin line they give me."

"Then that isn't an option either. Just show me what you can, and I'll take it from there."

He did. Three hours later, and I was a lot smarter when it came to photo manipulation software. Come to find out, it isn't just the big-name expensive software. There are other options out there too. And some side options that make the whole process a lot easier.

Like, did you know there is a free place online where you can go and completely remove the background from a picture? Neither did I. But now I do. And I plan on using it too. A lot.

It was hard to keep still on the drive home. I now knew just enough to be dangerous, as Mom used to say. And I was totally itching to try out my new-found skills. This would be a fun diversion after all. I just wish I had a little more time to do it right.

But I'd just have to make do with what I could do. Hopefully, that would be good enough.

My thoughts were on overdrive as I wound down our long driveway and back to the barn. The plan was coming together.

Then my heart about stopped as a cat dropped from a tree lining the drive and landed on my hood. The resulting swerve cost the car yet another scrape down the side. When I finally came to a dead stop, I was staring into Destiny's eyes. The only thing separating us was a thin glass windshield.

I jumped out of the car and stood staring at her with my fists on my hips. "What the bloody heck were you thinking? I could have killed you!"

She tilted her head at me, licked a paw, and rubbed the back of her ear. Just another walk in the park for her, obviously. She took her time, but when she finally finished, she hopped off the hood and started sauntering toward the house. She didn't get far before she looked over her shoulder to see if I was coming.

Crapsnackles. I hadn't added feeding her to the day's list.

Double Crapsnackles! The list! I'd totally forgotten to get groceries. I glanced at my watch. Arc would be home within the hour, and the drive into town and back would take more than half that time. Not to mention the whole shopping part of things. And the whole cooking thing.

"Meow!"

I was almost back in the car when Destiny sounded off. I hated making decisions. If I left now, I'd pay for it later. And most likely, poor little Yorkie Doodle would pay for it too. I couldn't have that.

I headed to the front door of the house at a dead run, grabbed the hidden key, and let us in. Then I headed straight to the cupboard, pulled out Destiny's food, filled her bowl and water dish, and scooped her litter. All in the space of like three minutes.

There was no way I was going to make this

work. Amie's fridge still didn't have any more in it than there had been yesterday, and now her freezer was pretty much bare too. There were a couple of packages far in the back, but they didn't look too trustworthy. I wasn't that desperate. Yet, anyway. Better to have dinner late to the table than to risk food poisoning.

I dashed into her pantry and started rambling. On the next to last shelf, I found my salvation. A box of spaghetti and a can of sauce. I could still pull this off.

But what to do about the whole garlic bread thing? Spaghetti just wasn't spaghetti without garlic bread.

I grabbed the box and can anyway and headed home. I'd come up with something. When I came in, Yorkie didn't greet me at the door like he normally did. It kind of had me worried. Worried enough that even in my current time crunch, I went looking for him.

He was hiding under my bed.

Lying flat on my belly, I looked him in the eyes. "What's the matter, Yorkie? Are you okay?"

He sniffed, and his tail slashed. I do believe that was the new universal dog language for Destiny.

"Was Destiny mean to you?"

He sniffed again. "Yip."

"I'm sorry, little guy. I really am. I'll have a talk with her, okay? She shouldn't take it out on you if

I forget to feed her." I patted the floor in front of me and Yorkie crawled out. "And I'll try really, really hard not to forget again, too, just in case, okay?"

I picked him up for a brief snuggle, and he licked my nose. A quick once over didn't show any wounds, so I was guessing that any lashing out that Destiny had done had been verbal. The cat could make anyone miserable with just her caterwauling. And my poor little dog had sensitive ears.

Yorkie got a free ride into the kitchen, and then I put him down to start dinner. I could still do this. But what about that darn bread?

Then I spotted the left-over hot dog buns. Hm. They would just have to do. I pulled out the tub of butter from the fridge and dumped two large scoops into a bowl, then I doused it with garlic powder and stirred it all up. Just like that, I had garlic butter to put on the hot dog buns. And if I spread the garlic butter on the inside part of the buns and toasted them in the oven... well, garlic toast.

I put the water on to boil and ran upstairs for a quick shower. That heat could really make a person sweat, and the little added fun after getting home hadn't really helped that issue. I didn't want Arc to get used to coming home and finding me a mess.

That wasn't a good plan to keep a man happy. Neither was running a shoddy kitchen, but I'd take care of that tomorrow. I'd make sure it made the top of the list again. And this time?

I was so taping that darn list to my steering wheel.

Chapter 7

When Arc got home, he seemed impressed by the wonderful Italian aroma coming from the kitchen. Of course, the impressed stage only lasted until he got a look at my quickly improvised garlic toast. But still, all in all, the dinner turned out rather well. If I did have to say so myself.

Maybe this cooking thing wasn't as bad as I made it out to be. I could so do this thing. And tomorrow, after my grocery run, when I really had food in the house? Well, it would only get easier, right?

After dinner, we settled in to watch a movie. Well, Arc settled in for the movie. I booted up my laptop. About halfway through his action-adventure flick, he finally noticed that I wasn't as enthralled with the film as he was and paused it.

"What are you doing?"

I chewed on the inside of my cheek for a minute before deciding to answer him. I really wanted to do this on my own, but I also kind of wanted to show off my new skill. It was pretty cool. Something like this could even get to be addicting after a while. Too bad I couldn't think of a single way to make money out of it. Well, other than blackmail, of course. And that just wasn't in my cards.

I started to turn the screen for him to see, then stopped. "First off, I want the same confidentially clause that you give to your clients at the firm. Nothing about any of this goes outside this house. Just you and me. Agreed?"

His eyes widened. "Now you really have my interest up. Agreed. Now, what's up?"

I showed him the screen and his eyes widened even more. Then he started laughing. "I really don't think Mayor Bradford ever looked that chiseled."

Frowning, I looked down at the screen. He had a point. I needed to make the images look realistic, and just switching out faces might not do that. I needed realistic looking bodies too. But that thought sent my heart into a tailspin. I was afraid that level of expertise was well beyond me.

Besides, I could get pictures of faces easy enough on the internet. But where on earth could I go to get pictures of naked bodies?

I know, I know. Duh, right? But I really didn't want to go to those virus-ridden websites. The last thing I needed was to ruin my poor little computer. I did a lot of important shopping on the thing.

"You can get all kinds of body images from a stock photography site."

Arc and I both jumped at the voice behind us. At least it wasn't just me.

"Sorry," Liz said. "Yorkie came over to visit and seemed to want me to walk him home. Patty is out with the pack, and I was bored, anyway. So I thought I'd check in with the two of you." She smiled and gave me a wink. "I made sure you both had your clothes on first, though."

Nice try, but how would she know whether we had clothes on if she hadn't looked? Not that I was going to call her on it. Being a ghost was hard enough as it was. Besides, it wasn't like she could knock.

After my immediate startlement faded, I looked at her. That's when I remembered that she'd been pretty well known for photography back when she... you know, wasn't a ghost. "Did you use this kind of software? Merging pictures and stuff?" There was a lot of hope hidden in that question.

"Sure. All the time. Sometimes for work. Sometimes just for fun. It's kind of addicting."

See? I was right.

Okay, so is it really getting help with a case, if that help was no longer living? I didn't think so. And that made Liz my perfect partner. I looked from her to the computer on my lap. "I know you can't actually work a computer anymore, but any chance you'd be willing to walk me through this?"

She grinned at me. "I'd love to!"

Her enthusiasm told me just how bored she really was. After all, she could never leave the estate. That would get tiring after a while on its own. Add in the whole not being able to use your hands, and it got bothersome quick.

We needed to come up with some way to keep her entertained. The page-turning mechanism that Lily had come up with to allow Liz to read wasn't nearly enough.

I glanced over at Arc. "Let's take this to the kitchen."

Arc raised an eyebrow at me. "This is sounding like more than a hobby or lark to you. What's going on?"

I gave him the sweetest smile I was capable of. "I'd love to tell you, but I'm working on a case. And, you know, there's that whole client confidentiality thing." Yeah, he had to know that would come back to bite him, eventually.

"Hey, I thought we were a team."

"We are. Usually, at least. But you're working long hours at the firm and even bringing work home. And yes, I saw how heavy your briefcase was tonight, so don't try to deny there's work in there. And with Amie gone, I needed something to distract myself."

"I'm not so sure I like the idea of you working alone to bring in a bond runner. That can be dangerous work." He hesitated. "Besides, I thought neither of our go-to bondsmen had any work this week."

His words made me even more sure that the reason I'd been told of the lack of work from both Boswell and Vincent was due to a little talk with Amie. I mean, come on. Perps don't just stop jumping bail because Amie goes out of town, do they?

Part of me wanted to let him stew on that. But he really looked worried. Besides, I didn't want him doing something stupid, like calling in the moms.

Reaching out, I patted his hand. "Don't you worry. This case isn't taking down a runner. It's more of an investigation thing." I hesitated, but then went ahead with a little more information. "It's kind of a local politics thing."

His eyes flew to the laptop. "You're going to blackmail the mayor?"

That got a laugh. "No, silly. But blackmail is involved. I'm trying to figure out a way around it, if all else fails." I motioned to the paused movie. "Go on back to your movie. Just be sure to remember everything I said tonight is under a very heavy confidentiality clause. And you happen to be the only one I've told, so I'll know if you break it. Just saying."

He swallowed but nodded. Mom was really kind of famous for her Karma spells. And I was my mother's daughter, after all. Arc wouldn't want to risk that. Not that I would actually do that to him. But as long as he didn't know that, he'd keep the secret.

Liz and I went to the kitchen counter. I noticed that the television volume went way down. I didn't think that was to help us concentrate, either. All the better to hear us with.

"So, what is it you're trying to do with the mayor?" Liz asked once we were settled. I was sitting on a barstool at the counter, and she was pretending to sit on the one next to me. Sometimes I had to wonder just how much concentration it took on her part to keep that illusion going. Probably quite a bit, but I appreciated the effort she put into it.

I glanced into the living room area. The movie was playing again, even if Arc was sitting up a little straighter than he usually did when resting and relaxing. I didn't plan to make eavesdropping easy on him.

Lowering my voice, I told her the basics of my plan.

"So, you plan to flood the market with doctored photos of local politicians and then leak the images to the press? You think Mabel will be happy with that?"

I shrugged. "I might have to run it by her before I drop the files off to the reporter, but yeah, I think she will. I mean, it's one thing to be singled out and blackmailed. But if a whole passel of politicians is being blackmailed, then, well, the blackmail wouldn't work, would it? I mean, everyone would know the images were fake, right?"

She nodded slowly. "I guess. So how long do we have to come up with the images?"

"A day and a half."

She just stared at me. "Please tell me you're kidding."

That didn't sound good. I shook my head. "Unfortunately not. Mabel doesn't want to risk the blackmailer making good on the threat." I hesitated. "I think she's more worried about Tommy seeing the photo than losing the chance of winning the election. But then again, if her boss at the library got wind of it, her days there would probably be numbered too. She works with a lot of kids there."

This was looking more and more like the kind of job I might not be able to pull off on my own.

Liz took pity on me. Probably because I'm pretty sure I looked like I felt. A kick in the teeth, even a well-meaning one, will do that to you. "Why don't you show me the pictures, and we'll go from there."

I pulled out the photos—I'd already taped them back together. I also had a couple of printouts of the blown-up tiny unicorn symbol. Wouldn't you know that little horned creature was the first thing that drew Liz's attention. I guess to her, naked bodies were a dime a dozen.

She looked from the unicorn to me, a huge grin on her face. "That symbol was in the bottom right corner of the image wasn't it?"

"Yes," I said slowly, drawing the word out. "I was told it's a kind of artist signature."

"Oh, it is." She paused for effect. "And I happen to know the artist."

Liz seemed to be a bit confused by my singular lack of excitement. "Yes, I guess they're pretty famous on the web. But without a name to go on, knowing their work doesn't really do us any good."

She laughed. "I wasn't saying I know their work. I know the unicorn herself. Name and all."

Now it was my turn to stare at her. She nodded toward the computer and rattled off a web address. I typed it in and hit enter. And just like that, my screen filled with spectacular images. The unicorn was very good at what she did. I was pretty sure a flight of dragons had never really done a flyover of New York City. Every image was perfect and seamless.

It kind of made putting one face over another seem like child's play.

"Why would someone with this kind of talent be trying to blackmail Mabel? Is the artist even local?"

Liz nodded. "She's in Oak Hill, actually." She frowned. "That's a whole county removed from Wind's Crossing. She wouldn't have any stake at all in the local election."

"Then she had to do this as a work for hire. I

hate to say it, but that doesn't paint too rosy of a picture of your friend the unicorn."

"Oh, I don't believe I called her a friend. She has been known to take on odd jobs from people needing mocked up documents and images. It isn't too far to go from a doctored college degree to something like this."

"She doctors college degrees?"

She shrugged. "I know of at least one she did. Not many people can afford her, though. She's not cheap."

I thought about the mini-mansion the Tanners lived in. Somehow, I didn't think money would be an issue. Not if it kept the cash flow... well, flowing.

"So, what's this unicorn's name? And does she have an office?"

Liz looked conflicted. "Her name is Britney, and no office. She works out of her home." She chewed for a minute on her lip. "You know one of your moms once said that it might be possible to get me out of the house and off the estate. I'd like to go with you on this one."

My feeling of shock must have been apparent on my face because she gave me a sad kind of chuckle. "No. I'm not blackmailing you. I'll give you her address and even directions to her house. But I do think it would be a good idea to take me along if it's something they can manage. Let's just say you might not get very far with Britney without me. She's pretty close-lipped about her... clients. She has to be."

I scratched my head, thinking. Then I glanced at the clock. It was still early enough to make the call.

"I'll see what I can do. And I'm really sorry we dropped the ball on getting you off the estate. We should have followed up on that by now. You could have reminded us, you know."

She nodded. "I know. But you all seem so busy all the time. And truthfully, my afterlife became so much more bearable after you all moved in. But now? Yeah, I'm getting a little restless again. It would be nice to be able to get out a little." She chuckled. "Said that lady that was a hermit in life."

Yeah, well, even hermits got out occasionally.

Chapter 8

Mom came through for us big time. She'd done the research for the spell months ago, but had then forgotten about it in all the crazy twists and turns our lives had taken in the past year. Hard to believe one family could have been through so much in such a short space of time.

But I guess that happens when the Goddess has big plans for your family. And her plans for us Ravenswinds were huge. Colossally huge. According to her, we were just getting started. And yes, it's possible to feel excited and dreadful all at the same time with news like that.

I didn't want to harvest anything from my newly planted garden quite this soon, so that meant a quick drive to Mom's house. It was totally worth it, even if it meant that the quick drive was followed by a rather lengthy visit. Lucky for me, it was a work night. So when the kids went up to bed, I said goodnight and headed out.

Mom followed me out to the car. I could tell

she had something to say. I could also tell it wasn't something she wanted to say. That had me worried.

"It was good seeing you tonight, Ruby."

"It was good seeing you, too, Mom. I'll try to make it back again for a longer visit soon. Plus, we have that cookout on the fourth. That is still a go, right?"

She nodded, but I could tell she was distracted. Her next words told me why. "Kimberly is working out great in the shop, but I could really use your help to stock up the potion supply. I've had to turn back of the shop customers away recently. I simply can't keep up."

Her words might not seem like all that big a deal. But then, that's because you don't know my mom like I do. She was asking for help. And that was something that Opal Ravenswind rarely did.

Even of her own daughter.

I'd been neglecting my mom in the worst way. When Kim had come into our lives, it had been like a get out of jail free card to me, and I'd taken it and ran. That shop might mean the world to Mom, but to me? It was just a job. And a boring one at that. I hadn't really considered that Kim would be of little help in the back room with the potions.

"Guess I didn't think about that. I'm sorry. I should have." I paused. "I'm working on something kind of important right now. But once that's handled, how's about I take a week off from bounty hunting, and we stock up those shelves again?"

She smiled at me. "That would be perfectly lovely, dear. And going forward?"

Yeah, stocking them up wouldn't last long if there were customers waiting, would it? "Would one day a week of concentrated brewing work for you? You could even pick the day." I gave her a conspiratorial grin. "If we're lucky, I can rope Amie into helping too, and we can get a heck of a lot done in a really short time."

"Her extra juice would make things go quicker, that's true. But let's keep that for the one day a week plan, if she's willing. I'd kind of like to have you to myself for that promised week, if you don't mind."

Funny, but when I'd been looking for something to do while Amie was away, this never crossed my mind. I was such a terrible daughter. Time to up my game here. Look at me, becoming the more well-rounded person.

"I'd like that too. Next week? Eight o'clock Monday morning?"

"See you then. Drive safe." Then she gave me a quick hug and walked back into the house. I owed Liz for more than just the help with Mabel's case.

Time to pay that back.

***

We saved the spell casting for the morning. Even though with it so close to hand, Liz was really chomping at the bit.

The trouble was, it wasn't an end-all, be-all spell. It had some major limitations. First of all, there was a distance limit. The spell wouldn't allow unlimited travel to wherever the spirit, namely Liz, wanted to go. The rough estimate on the spell's range was fifty miles from the haunting ground.

That would do for what we had in mind for today, but it would limit Liz's ability to travel. She wasn't as upset about that as I'd thought she'd be.

"Fifty miles? In any direction? That's huge." She gave me a chilly ghost hug, then stepped back as I shivered. "Sorry."

I grinned at her. "Don't be. Chilly feels nice right about now. You'll be great in the car. Give the air conditioning a break for a change." Then I hesitated ever so briefly. "There's a time limit too, I'm afraid. You get three hours, max."

Her teeth caught her bottom lip in a vise grip. "What happens if I'm not back at the end of the three hours?"

"Nothing major, according to the research Mom found. You'll simply be transported back here. Kind of like snapping a rubber band."

That, she didn't seem so sure about. I can't say I blamed her. The unknown was scary.

"Is there any way you could make sure to have

me back here in three hours? I don't want to rush you, but..."

"Don't worry. I get it. We'll be back well before that time is up."

She was okay with my answer, but she still looked sad.

"Is something wrong?"

Liz lifted one shoulder. "It's just that... well, I haven't been off the grounds for years. Three hours is such a short time. And I know you need my help, and I'm not complaining—not really, anyway—but there are a lot of places I'd rather go and people I'd rather see. You know?"

I nodded and grinned at her. Then I held up the satchel Mom had given me of spelling ingredients. "I know you can't feel how heavy this bag is, so you'll have to take my word on it. Mom stuffed it to the gills. The spell has limitations, yes. But nothing says we can't cast it more than once."

She bounced up and down. "Awesome. Could we cast it again at Britney's to give us more time?"

"Unfortunately, no. We'll still be limited to the three-hour window for this trip. But Mom said to tell you that she'll be back on the research for a more permanent and far-reaching spell. Hopefully, she'll find something soon."

Liz took a deep breath. At least, that's what she made it look like. "Well, if you're ready to go, then I am. Let's do this."

First things first, I took a countdown baking timer from the kitchen and set it for two hours and thirty minutes. Then I clipped it on the outside of my handbag. When it went off, we'd need to head home.

The spell only took a few seconds to mix and chant, and we were off.

Off to see the unicorn.

Chapter 9

There was a good reason why I was more than happy to have Liz with me for the trip. And it wasn't just for good company, though there was that too.

It wasn't because I thought she'd be an enormous help in getting the unicorn to talk to us either. I had a plan for that too. A plan I was pretty sure would work.

But in order for my plan to have its best shot at success, I had to dress in my full gear. My full bounty-hunting gear. Leather all the way. And wearing leather in late June isn't a very good idea. There may be some places on earth where you could get by with it. Alaska comes to mind. Most definitely not Michigan. We're north, but not that far north. It's hot here in the summer.

And that's where Liz came in super handy. It wasn't just the car's air conditioning that she was giving a break. It was me too. There were times we'd be out of the car, after all.

I timed the drive to Britney's. Twenty-five minutes and change. That gave us a maximum of two hours to do this before heading back. I glanced over at my mostly transparent traveling companion. Her eyes hadn't stopped moving the entire trip. Her conversation hadn't been exactly stellar either. Mostly confined to oohs and ah's and 'how long's that been there?'... that kind of thing.

"You ready to do this?" I asked her.

She nodded. "Is there a plan?"

I grinned at her. "Yup. I shouldn't really need you, but it's always a good idea to have a Plan B."

"Just call me B then."

We got out and walked up to the front door. The place was a modest little ranch home. Nothing ornate, but at least the outside was newly painted and kept up. That said a lot about the person inside to me.

When the door opened, I got my first shock. I hadn't expected Britney to live with her mother.

"That's her," Liz whispered. Though why she bothered to whisper, I didn't know. Unless the woman in front of us was a witch, too, she wouldn't be able to hear her even if she shouted. Or see her if she danced naked in her front yard for that matter. Not that I expected Liz to do that. But a free-roaming Liz was a more out-going Liz than what I was normally used to. So I was thinking nothing would surprise me right now.

Except, of course, the woman holding the door

open and giving me an odd look. She wasn't anything like I'd expected her to be.

"Britney Daniels?" I asked.

She nodded slowly, her eyes taking in my full gear. "Aren't you roasting in that getup? It's June, you know."

"Yes. I'm well aware. But I'm working, and this is kind of my uniform."

Britney arched an eyebrow at me. "And just what kind of work would that be?"

I angled my hips just enough to give the handcuffs a little jingle. Her eyes caught the movement and widened. "I think that's a conversation we should have inside. Don't you, Ms. Daniels?"

She glanced around and sure enough, the neighbor across the street had paused in watering her lawn to watch us with great interest. "Yes. I believe that might be best."

The front door gave way right into her main living room, so within a few short steps, we were all seated and looking at each other. Well, Britney and I were seated. Liz just kind of hovered around the room, taking everything in.

"Would you mind telling me what this is all about? And why you've shown up at my door with handcuffs? I hope you don't expect me to believe that you're the police. You aren't, and I wasn't born yesterday."

"No ma'am, I'm not the police. The police,

should they need to be brought into this, will come with a warrant. I can assure you of that."

Her eyes narrowed, but she said nothing. She was good, this woman.

But I was better. I let her stew. No way was I breaking the silence. One doesn't negotiate by being the first to break. And if there is one thing I'm a master at, it's negotiation.

It didn't take long, either. "And may I ask what you are referring the police might be brought into?"

I gave her a slow smile. "I think you know what I'm referring to. Now, don't you?"

Her eyes shifted slightly, but the woman was a rock. She didn't lose her cool or break like I'd kind of hoped. "I'm afraid I don't have a clue. You'll have to enlighten me."

She was very good. She almost had me believing her. Almost.

I took one of the printouts of the unicorn logo from my bag. "I believe you will recognize this logo? A digital signature, I believe they call it?"

She hesitated for the briefest of seconds. "I'll ask again if need be. What is this all about?"

"Oh, nothing earth-shattering. Just fraud, counterfeiting legal documents, and blackmail."

Britney gasped. "Blackmail? I never!"

"Well, if you never, then one of your clients did, Ms. Daniels. And I have the images in my bag with your little logo in the corner. Quite a distinctive little unicorn. Very original, I have to say."

For the first time, she seemed a little nervous. Even now, when she knew the cards I was holding, she kept her cool. This woman was very, very good.

"So, I'm going to ask you a direct question, Ms. Daniels, and it would greatly benefit you to be upfront and honest with me. But before I do that, I will tell you that I'm not here about you. I'm here about your client. That could change if I don't get the help I need."

I hadn't asked my question yet, but I waited all the same. Finally, she gave me a small nod. "I'm listening."

"Is this your business logo?" I pointed to the tiny purple and gold dancing unicorn.

"It is. Though I should point out that it could easily be copied and inserted into images."

"It could. But that argument rather loses its strength if the copier makes it so hard to find, now doesn't it?"

She squared her shoulders. "Not necessarily."

"I see." I took a deep breath and stood. "I'd hoped not to bring all this out and into the open, but if that's what it takes to get my answers in a straightforward manner, then that's what I guess I have to do."

I didn't even get fully turned to the door.

"Wait," she said. "You really aren't interested

in me? Can I have a guarantee of that?"

"I have interest only in the blackmail case at this point. I have no direct knowledge of any wrongdoing on your part. Are we clear?"

She thought about it and then nodded slowly. "If you show me the images, and I tell you who ordered the work, you leave and never come back?"

"If I leave here with everything I need to stop the blackmailer, then yes. To a point. If I get hired by another client and the path leads to your door, I may however return."

But what were the chances of that happening, right? Still, I thought it important enough to mention. One never knew what the future held.

***

My step was a whole lot lighter by the time we left Britney's house. Things were coming together nicely.

I had what I needed to confront the Tanners, and I was well on the way to proving myself a competent woman. All in all, things were definitely going my way.

We left her house with plenty of time to reach the safety of Liz's haunting grounds too. At least, that's what we thought at the time. With a full thirty minutes to make a twenty-five-minute drive, it shouldn't have been any sweat, right?

But then we had to stop for a long train and lost five full minutes. It made things a lot closer, but still doable. Liz didn't look too worried. A little concerned maybe, but not really worried.

Until we got behind the huge farm equipment, going thirty miles below the speed limit.

"We aren't going to make it," she said. There was a lot more than just concern in her voice.

I tried to pass three times, and each time another car was coming, and I had to pull back behind him again. "You know, according to Mom's research, you'll be fine even if we don't make it back. You'll just snap back there, that's all." I just wish my words sounded a little more sure of themselves. Liz's worry was catching.

On the fourth try, I got around him. I think it's safe to say that my car didn't go a single mile under the speed limit the rest of the way. We were about a half-mile away from our driveway when Liz gasped. "Ruby, I don't feel so good. I'm not sure your mom was right about that snapping thing. That would just be an instant thing, right?"

I swallowed and floored it.

Belinda White

Chapter 10

"Hold on, Liz. I think we can make it!"

We'd reset the timer before we left Oak Hill. Back when we thought we had plenty of time. I was kind of wishing now that we'd saved those precious few seconds. But at least with the timer, we knew just how close we were on time.

Seconds away.

I turned into the driveway going way too fast, and when the tires hit the gravel, I kind of lost control of the car there for a few seconds. We'd need a new mailbox, but that didn't really matter to me right at the moment.

All that really mattered was that at least the front half of the car—and more importantly, its ghostly occupant—was on that drive as the timer went off.

When I finally came to a stop with the car actually on the driveway, I turned to Liz. "You okay?"

Her eyes were still a bit wild, but she nodded.

"Yeah. But man, that was a little too close for comfort."

Yeah, not what I had wanted at all for her first time out. It might be a long time before she agreed to leave the comfort of her haunting grounds again. I'd really wanted her to go with me to see the Tanners. But I wasn't sure that would be an option.

"We'll need to plan a little more leeway to get back after we visit the Tanners," Liz said.

Or maybe it was an option after all.

"You sure you're up to another trip? I would totally understand if you weren't."

She thought for a minute. "I'll be okay. But I would like a few minutes to recuperate before we do the spell and head back out." She glanced over at me with a mischievous smile. "Besides, I think maybe Destiny wants a word with you."

Liz turned to look at the house, and I followed the path of her gaze. Destiny was sitting in one of the big picture windows staring out at the car. And I could see her tail slashing the air from here.

I was in so much trouble. Liz floated off to check on the estate, and I went in to face the music.

After letting myself in, I turned to the angry feline. "I know, and I'm sorry. But let's face it, there's still food in your bowl, right? And water in your dish? And you didn't really go to the bathroom so much that your litter box is all that bad, now did you?" I looked her dead in her angry eyes. "So get over it. If you're nice, then I'll bring you over some of the leftovers from our dinner tonight as a treat. I'm planning to cook."

She tilted her head and just looked at me.

"Yes, actually cook. And not hot dogs or spaghetti with stale hot dog buns doubling as garlic toast either. A proper meal." I glanced at Amie's kitchen wall clock after re-filling Destiny's dishes. As I'd thought, neither was empty. The day wasn't even halfway gone yet.

I so had this.

First the spell on Liz, and then the confrontation with the Tanners. That still should give us plenty of time for us to run into the market at Wind's Crossing and pick up a cart full of food.

Yes, I wish I had a grocery list, but there wasn't really time to make one out right now. I'd just have to wing it.

***

It only took twenty minutes to make it to the Tanners. Guess we were a little closer to Wind's Crossing than we were to Oak Hill. Five minutes closer to be exact. And yes, we brought along our handy little timer. I set it to go off a full forty minutes before the three-hour window. Plenty of time to get home with lots of minutes left.

And that gave us two entire hours to deal with

the Tanners and stock up on food. So doable.

We sat there and looked at the house for a full minute, gathering our thoughts.

"I suppose you have a plan for this one too? Can't see how I'll be much help on this one." She grimaced. "Not that I turned out to be much help on the last one either."

I grinned at her. "Oh, you're tons of help."

"I am? How? Moral support?" She gave me a crooked grin. "Should I do your little cheer again?"

"No need. I know you have my back. But you really help with the whole temperature thing. I really need my leather for this, and it's June. In Michigan."

Her eyes grew big. "Oh."

"Yeah. Oh, is right. You're practically an essential for these trips. I really appreciate your help."

Her smile was a lot more genuine now. But I meant every word.

We got out and walked up to the front door. I rang the bell and waited. It didn't take long.

Mrs. Tanner opened the door with a huge smile. "Oh, hello again! You're in luck, Mr. Tanner is home…" Her words trailed off as her eyes went from my face to my outfit. "Are those handcuffs?"

Funny how some people focused on the handcuffs. Me? My eyes would be totally focused on the other side of my hips. Where the taser holster was.

"As a matter of fact, yes, they are. And it's a very good thing that Mr. Tanner is home because I need to speak with the both of you."

She hesitated.

"I really think you will want to listen carefully to what I have to say, Mrs. Tanner."

Finally, the door opened, and we were in.

Mr. Tanner stood from the sofa with a big smile. He must not have heard the bit about the handcuffs. Probably still thought I was there to tell them when their new fridge would be delivered. Surprise!

"Please, don't stand on my account, Leroy." I was done with the formalities here. The only reason I'd called Mrs. Tanner by her proper name was because for the life of me I couldn't remember what her first name was. If I'd ever even known it. "I'm thinking this won't take long."

Mrs. Tanner gave him a worried look and then sat down next to him. I stayed on my feet for this one.

I held up the brown envelope with the fake images of Mabel. "You might recognize this, Mrs. Tanner. You sent it to a friend of mine. I might be making assumptions here, but you do realize that blackmail is illegal, don't you?"

Leroy's eyes went to his wife. "Kathrine, what have you done now?"

Her eyes flared as she looked back at him. "Well, at least I did something. You aren't even campaigning anymore. Do you know how close you are to losing against that… that… librarian? Do you know what we stand to lose?"

He shook his head and repeated himself. "What have you done?"

Her lips thinned, and she crossed her arms in front of her. A stone wall of a woman. A non-talking stone wall of a woman.

That was fine with me. I had no problem answering his question.

"She ordered some doctored photos of your opponent. You know, like some of the ones you have here?" I motioned to the photos lining the mantel in a place of honor. Yeah. All fake. "Only these images were particularly nasty. She was using them to blackmail Ms. Morgan into dropping out of the political race."

His eyes went from me to his wife. Kathrine, that was her name. I'd need to remember that. "Is this true?"

She smirked. An actual smirk. But then she didn't know what else the envelope in my hand now held. It was quite a bit fatter now.

"She's blowing smoke, Leroy. She can't prove any of this."

I gave her a big smile with lots of teeth showing. "Actually, that's not an accurate statement. And just so you know… these are copies. I have the originals in a very safe place."

Then I opened the packet and spread the images on the coffee table in front of them. First the headless pictures of the not-Mabel, then the blown-up version of the unicorn symbol in the corner of that image. Next came one of the pictures of Leroy with a past president. And the blown-up version showing the unicorn symbol in the corner of that one as well. Next, a screenshot of Britney's website with the same logo.

"Ha. Good luck with this," Kathrine said with a little smile. "Anyone could have found her site and ordered those photos. There is nothing here to say it was me. We just used the same company, that's all."

"You might think that, but you'd be wrong. Turns out, this isn't a company, but an individual. An individual who, as it turns out, feels very strongly about her work being used for blackmail. I have a copy of the order you placed, by the way. A copy of the payment receipt too."

I paused to let that sink in. "You know the order you emailed her telling her of the crush Leroy has on Ms. Morgan, and that nasty little fantasy you wanted to help him with?"

"Kathrine!" Leroy didn't look amused.

She closed her eyes for a minute, then opened them and stared at me. "That really doesn't change anything, though, does it? Mabel won't risk those pictures being distributed, and I still have copies. Plus, you try to prove any of this with the authorities, and they get used as evidence. She won't agree to that. Stalemate." She leaned back, looking a lot more self-confident than she had any right to.

Because I wasn't finished yet.

"I was afraid that might be your reaction." I pulled the last images out of the envelope and placed them on top of the others. A college degree from Princeton University. And yet another blown up unicorn emblem. Then I just stood there, watching them.

Leroy looked at the degree and gave a big swallow. "What do you want?"

Yeah, it was that serious. Universities like Princeton took a very dim view of people forging degrees from them. Lawsuits, publicity that definitely wasn't good for you, criminal charges… a whole passel of trouble.

"I want every single copy of the doctored image of Mabel, and I want the email with the doctored image attachment permanently deleted. No hard copies, no digital copies to remain. Is that clear?"

He nodded, then elbowed his wife. It took a minute, and she wasn't happy about it, but finally, she gave a curt nod too.

"Mabel has nothing to do with this part of things. But if a single image of her is released to anyone—and I mean anyone—I will take the counterfeit degree public. And I'll have no choice but to release the copy of that emailed order too. I'm sure the voting public would be highly interested in Leroy's sexual fantasies regarding Ms. Morgan. Might just turn the tide in her favor, now that I think about it."

Color rose on Leroy's cheeks as he glared at his wife. "You have my word that won't happen."

"Good." I gathered up the images and put them back in the envelope, minus the headless originals. Those were coming with me. The envelope, I was leaving for them. As I'd said, I had copies of everything at home. "I'm glad we understand each other."

I waited for her to gather the other copies for me, and even watched while she deleted the email from the unicorn. That done, I turned to leave, but I just couldn't resist one last barb.

"Oh, and Kathrine? I think I'd be planning to buy my own appliances from here on out if I were you."

Belinda White

Chapter 11

All that done, and we were only at the Tanner's for less than thirty minutes. An hour and a half of free time left.

I glanced over at the still giggling Liz. We'd both had a good laugh when we pulled away from the Tanner curb. It felt good. Really, really good.

"Would you mind terribly if we stopped off at the library to give Mabel the good news? I don't want to run the risk of her pulling out of the race early because I didn't get to her in time."

Liz gave a little bounce. "The library? Oh, that would be lovely!" Then she paused. "You do have a card, don't you? And would you mind checking out a few books for me?"

"Yes, I have a card, and no, I wouldn't mind." In fact, I felt a little guilty about not offering to get her any books that she might want before this. I guess I just assumed that if she wanted something, she'd ask.

That didn't seem to be the case with Liz.

Once inside the building, Liz floated off in search of her next reads, and I headed straight to Mabel. She looked over her shoulder, then at me. "He's in today," she whispered.

I thought quick. "Could you help me find this book, please? I'm a little rusty on the library's search function." I made sure to talk a little louder than my normal tone. I wanted to make sure her boss heard my request.

"Sure, I can help you." Mabel stepped out from behind the counter, and we walked over to the public access computer. Far enough away from the office for privacy. As soon as we were there, she glanced over at me. "I've decided to drop out. It's just too risky."

"Please tell me you haven't set that in motion yet! I've taken care of it."

The look she gave me told me she didn't have a lot of confidence in my words. I pulled out the envelope and passed it to her. The degree and the Tanner images were all still at their house. That was between me and the Tanners. My little insurance policy. But all the copies of Mabel were right there for her to destroy at her leisure.

"It was Kathrine Tanner. All the doctored images with your face are here. Physical and digital. And I personally watched her delete the email from her computer too. You're in the clear. Plus, I have their word this is done."

She shook her head. "Sorry, but why would they go to all this trouble, and then just give up? I don't trust them. Well, I never trusted Leroy, but now doubly so."

"Oh, I don't trust their word, either. But I have a bit of surety that they'll keep it this time. While I did my little investigation, I got some pretty dang hard stuff on old Leroy. Stuff he and his wife really wouldn't want to come out." After all, an election was one thing, lawsuits and possible jail time was another.

Mabel frowned at me. "You mean you're blackmailing them?"

I thought about my wording carefully. "I don't consider it blackmail. I think it's more... an added consequence if they decide to do something dastardly."

She took a deep breath and finally nodded. "I suppose that's all right then. At least you're not trying to gain from it, right?"

"Exactly. No gain at all."

"And you're one hundred percent positive these are all the images?" She hesitated. "Couldn't they just get another copy from the person who did them?"

"Nope. That door is firmly shut to them too. You're safe, Mabel." I laid my hand on her arm. "And we need Leroy out of that office."

"Yes, we do." There was movement out of the

corner of my eye. I pointed to the screen. "Are those the only books you have on that?"

She looked at me, then caught the glimpse of her boss at the door to his office. "Yes. Follow me, and I'll take you to them." Mabel reached out and pushed the home button on the computer, then led us away out into the stacks.

I could think of another great reason for Mabel to get elected. Her boss wasn't the nicest man to work for. But we'd sure as heck miss her here. He didn't realize how many people came to this library because of Mabel. He'd realize it once she got elected for sure.

She led me out to the middle of the library, pointed to a random shelf, and then whispered, "Thank you, Ruby."

"Anytime Mabel. Just win, okay?"

Mabel smiled and then left me. I stood there for a minute pretending to study the books in front of me, just in case. Even took one of them for good measure. It was a book on gardening, so who knows? It might come in handy after all.

I followed Liz around the library for another hour before I finally had to rein her in. Besides, I could barely hold all the books she'd already pointed out.

By the time we checked out and made it out to the car, we had less than a half-hour before the timer went off.

"Sorry I took so much time in there. It's just

been so long..."

"No worries. We still have time for a quick trip to the market. I'll just get what I need for a few days. I didn't have time to make a list anyway, so I'd be bound to forget something."

Liz watched the other people and oohed and ahhed at all the new products on the shelves as I loaded down my cart. People she'd never get to speak to or interact with, and products that she'd never get to try. It didn't seem one bit fair to me.

I really hoped her rat of a murderer was having a rough time in prison. The rougher the better, as far as I was concerned.

We moved at a good clip, and I filled my cart in just under our time limit. There were hamburgers, steaks, chicken strips, and all the fixings to go with them. Three nutritious meals right there. Plus, a good stock-up of soda, snacks, and a case of Arc's favorite beer. I was kind of hoping to save the steaks for the weekend and let Arc fix them on the grill. I really didn't want to mess up a good steak.

Tonight would be an easy one. Barbecued chicken, mashed potatoes, and asparagus. My stomach growled just thinking of it. That's when I realized that with all of our running, I hadn't stopped for lunch. And I didn't want to take the time now to go through the drive-thru.

I'd run a little too close on time with our first outing. Twice in a row wouldn't be a good thing for

Liz's confidence in me.

Chapter 12

By the time Arc was due home, I'd already feed Destiny her nightly meal and freshly scooped her box. I'd also watered my newly planted garden, taken Yorkie for a well-deserved walk around the estate, and fixed a wonderful and nutritious dinner.

I was proud of myself. And with good reason.

In the three days I'd been on my own, I had helped a friend in need, planted the start of a nice little witch's garden, given my ghost friend a new lease on life (well, afterlife), and still managed to get the shopping done and dinner made.

That's a lot.

Amie and Opie would be back tonight, and that was great. Even as busy as I'd been, I had still missed her. She was a big part of my life and always would be.

But I had a feeling that things might be a little

different between us from here out. In a good way.

I'd never really been on my own before. I had gone from living at home to sharing a home with Arc. And from working for Mom to working with Amie.

Not that I ever wanted to give any of that up, mind you. I loved my family. They're dang awesome, and it means a lot to know that they'll always have my back.

No matter what life throws at us. Shoot, we've already proven that.

But independence was a brand new feeling to me. And I liked it.

And who really cares if I burnt the asparagus just a little? I really doubted Arc would even notice.

I'm calling it a win.

A Familiar Epilogue

(From Yorkie Doodle)

"You know she thinks she did this all on her own, right?" Destiny asked.

"Yip." I knew. And I didn't really care, either.

"You don't care, either, do you?"

Like I said, nope. "Yip, yip."

"You're such a dog."

"Yip." Thanks for the compliment. Glad you noticed.

Destiny rolled her eyes at me. She understood me. Just like I understood her. It was kind of nice having someone to talk to finally. The humans didn't get my language. Not sure why. I got theirs. Human is much harder to learn than dog. Just sayin'.

They might not be as smart as they think they are. And a lot of them think dogs are dumb. Not my human, of course, but some humans think that.

"Do you think her plan would have worked if

97

you hadn't brought over Liz when you did?"

I lifted a shoulder. "Yip." Who knew? "Yip, yip." Ruby was more resourceful than the others gave her credit for. Especially when it came to helping out a friend.

"Well, maybe you're right. But if it hadn't been for the constant reminders, she'd have let me starve, for sure."

That didn't even get a yip. Just a look. No way was Destiny going to starve, and she knew it. Shoot, she ate almost as much of my kibble as I did.

"I do think you cowering under the bed like that and then blaming it on me was a bit much though."

"Yip."

"Yeah, I know, it worked. To a point."

I lifted my nose to the deliciously scented breeze wafting by us. Yip, but those steaks smelled like a sunny day at the dog park.

"Think they're gonna share?"

"Yip."

Destiny laughed. "Yeah, you're right. Like we're gonna give them a choice."

"Yip, yip."

"Okay, okay, I'll let Mom know the food's about ready."

Baxter, Destiny's mom, was Arc's familiar. I liked her well enough, but I couldn't understand a darn thing she said. Just like she couldn't understand me. She was nice enough for a feline, but she kind of kept to herself most of the time.

Didn't feel right to leave her out of the whole steak thing, though. A rare occasion like this needed to be shared by all of us familiars.

I was really hoping this thing with Ruby cooking would last. I kind of liked it.

There's so much more to life than just kibble.

A Note From Belinda

Thank you so much for reading Ruby's very first novella. I had a lot of fun with this one. (Hopefully, you could tell!)

There's a funny story about this one. I fully intended for this to be a short story. As a short, I was going to put it in the Gemstone Coven Holiday Shorts Series. Yeah. Several thousand words later and the story was just getting good. So, it ended up as a short novella instead. And Ruby Ravenswind got her very own series.

I'm truly hoping that you enjoyed reading it as much as I enjoyed writing it.

If you have a spare minute or two, I'd greatly appreciate it if you could leave me a short review. I'd love to know what you thought of the story!

Belinda White
July 2020

Made in the USA
Columbia, SC
13 November 2023

26179407R00062